Muddled-up Farm

Written by Mike Dumbleton Illustrated by Jobi Murphy

Star Bright Books
Cambridge, Massachusetts

For Ruby and Abigail, with love. M.D.

For Paul, with many thanks to Linsay, Bully and Seb. J.M.

Originally published in Australia in 2002 by Red Fox, an imprint of Random House Australia Pty., Ltd.

First published in the United States of America in 2013 by Star Bright Books, Inc. The name Star Bright Books and the Star Bright Books logo are registered trademarks of Star Bright Books, Inc.

Please visit www.starbrightbooks.com.
For bulk orders, please email: orders@starbrightbooks.com, or call customer service at: (617) 354-1300

Hardback ISBN-13: 978-1-59572-630-8
Star Bright Books / MA / 00103130
Printed in China / Toppan / 10 9 8 7 6 5 4 3 2 1

Paperback ISBN-13: 978-1-59572-631-5
Star Bright Books / MA / 00103130
Printed in China / Toppan / 10 9 8 7 6 5 4 3 2 1

Library of Congress Cataloging-in-Publication Data

Dumbleton, Mike.
 Muddled-up Farm / written by Mike Dumbleton ; illustrated by Jobi Murphy.
    p. cm.
 Summary: "On Muddled-up Farm everything is mixed up! The cat says moo, and the cow meows. The goat goes woof and the chickens neigh. When a farm inspector visits he tries to get everything right but things don't go as he planned!"-- Provided by publisher.
 ISBN 978-1-59572-630-8 (hardcover) -- ISBN 978-1-59572-631-5 (pbk.)
 [1. Farms--Fiction. 2. Domestic animals--Fiction. 3. Animal sounds--Fiction. 4. Humorous stories.] I. Murphy, Jobi, ill. II. Title.
 PZ7.D89355Mu 2013
 [E]--dc23
                         2012020093

On a hill far away,

with its own special charm, is

a wonderful place

called . . .

Muddled-up Farm.

On Muddled-up Farm
the cat says . . .

"moo."

And a pig
on the fence
calls . . .

"cock-a-
doodle-doo."

The goat goes . . .

"woof,"

and the chickens say . . .

"nei

The horse drinks . . .

milk,

and the cat
chews . . .

But when a farm inspector
arrived from town,
he didn't look pleased;
he spoke with a frown.

"This is all very strange.

There is cause for alarm.

It can't be allowed!

This is not a proper farm."

"I don't know what's happened
but it's gone too far.
A dog's got to woof
and a sheep's got to baa!"

"I'll teach every one of you

what to say.

I'll start with the chickens—

I'll start right away."

So he **clucked** at the chickens.

And he

mooed

at the cow.

But the cow just looked

at him and said . . .

He worked
with the
animals day and night.
Then he finally announced
they were saying things right.

"At last you sound as animals should. Muddled-up Farm is fixed for good."

The inspector glared

and his face went red.

Then he tried to speak

but he **quacked** instead.

He quacked and he baaed,

and he **woofed**

and he **mooed.**

Then he jumped up on the fence . . .

and he

cock-a-
doodle-dooed!